GOOD ADVICE FROM A PLAYER

William T. Golson, Jr.

Order this book online at www.trafford.com
or email orders@trafford.com

Most Trafford titles are also available at major online book retailers.

Note for Librarians: A cataloguing record for this book is available from Library and Archives Canada at www.collectionscanada.ca/amicus/index-e.html

Printed in Victoria, BC, Canada.

ISBN: 978-1-4269-1474-4 (Soft)

We at Trafford believe that it is the responsibility of us all, as both individuals and corporations, to make choices that are environmentally and socially sound. You, in turn, are supporting this responsible conduct each time you purchase a Trafford book, or make use of our publishing services. To find out how you are helping, please visit www.trafford.com/responsiblepublishing.html

Our mission is to efficiently provide the world's finest, most comprehensive book publishing service, enabling every author to experience success. To find out how to publish your book, your way, and have it available worldwide, visit us online at www.trafford.com

Trafford rev. 9/3/2009

www.trafford.com

North America & international
toll-free: 1 888 232 4444 (USA & Canada)
phone: 250 383 6864 • fax: 812 355 4082 • email: info@trafford.com

CONTENTS

ACKNOWLEDGEMENTS

I thank the following friends and relatives who read, reviewed, and gave me constructive comments and recommendations: Flo Callaway. Rev. B. Mark Francis, and my daughter in-law Ashley Golson

INTRODUCTION

1 Kings 11:3 tells us that King Solomon was one who was quite the sport, "He had 700 hundred wives, princesses, and 300 hundred concubines." He was in anyone's estimation the ultimate womanizer or what might be called the ultimate player. The Funk and Wagnall's dictionary defines the term "player" as *n.* 1. One who participates in a game or sport. 2. One who performs in theatrical roles; actor. In street vernacular, one who is a player is one who makes a sport of romanticizing, or having a variety of relationships with numerous women, typically with the goal of personal gain.

Sometimes it is just for the sport, that is, because they can. Sometimes it is for the economics involved, that is, like a gigolo, the support provided, and sometimes for the release of sexual tension and fulfillment. However, no modern definition would consider a player to be wise and certainly not one to emulate.

Interestingly, in spite of his womanizing, it is said of Solomon that he was the wisest man on the earth. 1 Kings 4:29-30 declares of Solomon,

> *"And God gave Solomon wisdom and exceedingly great understanding, and largeness of heart like the sand on the seashore. Thus Solomon's wisdom excelled the wisdom of all the men of the East and all the wisdom of Egypt."*

The Queen of Sheba having met with him was so impressed with his display of wealth and wisdom she was led to proclaim in 1 Kings 10:1-7:

1 *Now when the queen of Sheba heard of the fame of Solomon concerning the name of the Lord, she came to test him with hard questions.*
2 *She came to Jerusalem with a very great retinue, with camels that bore spices, very much gold, and precious stones; and when she came to Solomon, she spoke with him about all that was in her heart.*
3 *So Solomon answered all her questions; there was nothing so difficult for the king that he could not explain it to her.*
4 *And when the queen of Sheba had seen all the wisdom of Solomon, the house that he had built,*
5 *the food on his table, the seating of his servants, the service of his waiters and their apparel, his cupbearers, and his entryway by which he went up to the house of the Lord, there was no more spirit in her.*
6 *Then she said to the king: "It was a true report which I heard in my own land about your words and your wisdom.*
7 *"However I did not believe the words until I came and saw with my own eyes; and indeed the half was not told me. Your wisdom and prosperity exceed the fame of which I heard.*

However, in spite of all his fame, wealth, and wisdom, he had an achilles heel. Women were his pleasure and women were his downfall. They influenced him down a path of gradual compromise. 1 Kings 11:3-4 tells us,

> *"His wives turned away his heart. For it was so, when Solomon was old, that his wives turned his heart after other gods; and his heart was not loyal to the Lord his God, as was the heart of his father David."*

Regardless of his personal failings, we find in scripture two significant works attributed to his writings: Proverbs and the Songs of Solomon. It is clear, probably in reflection, that he understood the temptations as well as the joys of female relationships.

In Proverbs 18:22 he makes a rather profound statement. Contrary to the multitude of relationships in his personal life, he advises the reader, *"He who finds a wife finds a good thing, and obtains favor from the Lord."*

In a country such as ours that devalues monogamy, where for many couples living together is preferred to marriage, where there is much gender confusion, and where the definition of marriage is being challenged, one has to wonder about Solomon's advice. Solomon's lifestyle would seem to be aligned more with the societal customs of our day; yet, we find him making a statement that is reflective of a different time and moral standard. What are we to think of this advice from a player? The advice would seem to be credible, but the advisor suspect.

Many singles in our society are struggling with the matter of marriage, or for that matter finding a meaningful relationship with the opposite sex. Often in desperation, depression, and loneliness some are given to compromise. What are they to think of this advice from a player? It appears that Solomon knew none of the emotional dilemmas that modern singles are confronted with. He was not only financially advantaged, but also advantaged in relationship.

Some who may be of a "Solomon spirit", a player spirit, may question if Solomon had just grown weary. Had he become disenchanted with having had a multiplicity of relationships? Is his advice the result of burnout, old age, possibly impotency, or had he come to this conclusion while yet passionate about love, romance, and sexual fulfillment? What are they to think of this advice from a player?

There are many who would advise us: friends, family, coworkers, professional counselors, authors, radio, and television personalities. Our underlying assumption is that those who would advise us are credible people, who having an ample amount of self-control, are not presently under the influence or addiction of the maladies we are presently facing. Admittedly, there is surely wisdom to be gained from those who have gone through what we have gone through. However, the magnitude of Solomon's insatiable desire for intimate companionship causes us to wonder. Can his intoxication with the opposite sex give way to the exercise of wisdom, and if so, on what terms? At first glance, the advice Solomon gives, is a toxic mixture of women and wisdom.

If you are single, or in a significant relationship, and have a "player" spirit, the hope is that, this book will assist you in the consideration of a mate from a biblical perspective. Moreover, that you will come to see that marriage is of real benefit to you personally and spiritually.

For those of you who are married, the hope is that this book will cause you to reflect upon the quality and foundation of your relationship, affirm your marriage as a covenant relationship with God, and recognize in fulfilling your commitments to each other you will experience His divine favor reflected in your relationship and lives.

Chapter 1

IS SOLOMON'S ADVICE CREDIBLE?

Although Solomon's life was not perfect, we can receive his wisdom with confidence because truth is truth even if told by a fool.

"Listen, my son, to your father's instruction and do not forsake your mother's teaching." (Proverbs 1:8)

We live in a time when we have at our disposal a multitude of advice. Everybody has advice: Oprah, Dr. Phil, Dr. Laura, the Today Show, Republicans, Democrats, Liberals, preachers, teachers, straight, gay, and lesbian. The problem, if a problem exists, is that we have too much advice. How do we know which advice to take? How do we know which path to pursue?

Solomon is declared to have been one of the wisest men on earth. However, when we look at the life of Solomon the number of wives, princesses, and concubines it seems that he had, at least in his later years, somewhat of a player spirit in his heart. He had an insatiable desire for the company and pleasures of the opposite sex, and surrounded himself with riches. He would be considered the Hugh Hefner of Playboy fame, or the Donald Trump of his day. This same Solomon wrote the majority of the book of Proverbs, the book of wisdom, the book of advice, if you will. When we read the book of Proverbs, we read bits and pieces of wisdom from supposedly one of the wisest men who ever lived on earth. Therein, we find a generous body of advice regarding divine ethics, politics, and economics. Solomon exposes vices, recommends virtues, and suggests rules for the control of ourselves in all relationships, conditions, and turns of life.

The question is; can we get credible advice from someone like a Solomon? Can we separate his life from his words and find meaning and constructive wisdom to live our lives? Can we get good advice from a player?

SOLOMON WAS THE WISEST OF MEN

> *"And God gave Solomon wisdom and exceedingly great understanding, and largeness of heart like the sand on the seashore. Thus Solomon's wisdom excelled the wisdom of all the men of the East and all the wisdom of Egypt." (1 Kings 4:29-30)*

The story is told of an angel appearing at a faculty meeting and telling the dean that in return for his unselfish and exemplary behavior, the Lord will reward him with his choice of infinite wealth, wisdom, or beauty. Without hesitating, the dean selects infinite wisdom. "Done!" says the angel, and disappears in a cloud of smoke and a bolt of lightning. Now, all heads turn toward the dean, who sits surrounded by a faint halo of light. After a period of silence, one of his colleagues whispers, "Say something wise." The dean looks at them and says, "I should have taken the money."

The Scriptures tell us that like the dean Solomon was given an opportunity to ask for whatever he wanted. In 1 Kings 3:5, God appeared to Solomon in a dream and extended to him the granting of the request of his heart. Solomon feeling the weight and enormity of succeeding his father David as king asked for the ability to judge between right and wrong; or what we would simply deem wisdom. Solomon said, *"Therefore give to Your servant an understanding heart to judge Your people, that I may discern between good and evil. For who is able to judge this great people of Yours?"* (1 Kings 3:9)

God was so pleased with Solomon's request that he granted him wisdom and more. In verse 12 and 13 of that third chapter God says,

> *"Behold, I have done according to your words; see, I have given you a wise and understanding heart, so that there has not been anyone like you before you, nor shall any like you arise after you. And I have also given you what you have not asked: both riches and honor, so that there shall not be anyone like you among the kings all your days."*

Unlike the dean, Solomon had no "wish" remorse. He received both wisdom and riches. Solomon was one who experienced great favor of God. He had it all: wisdom, fame, and money. People came from near and far just to sit at his feet and hear what he had to say.

As with the dean, given an opportunity to ask for anything that you wanted, what would you have asked for? Perhaps you would have been like one of the three women who found a bottle by the side of the road. Three women were walking down a street and found a bottle lying on the side of the road. They picked it up and a genie popped out. The genie said, "You will each get one wish." The first woman wished she were 20 times smarter. The genie made her 20 times smarter. The second woman wished she were 30 times smarter. The genie made her 30 times smarter. The last woman wished she were 60 times smarter. The genie turned her into a man.

The best we can imagine of ever having an opportunity like this is in a joke, but it was a reality for Solomon when God gave him a blank check.

SOLOMON HAD A CHARACTER FLAW

> *"But King Solomon loved many foreign women, as well as the daughter of Pharaoh: women of the Moabites, Ammonites, Edomites, Sidonians, and Hittites—from the nations of whom the Lord had said to the children of Israel, "You shall not intermarry with them, nor they with you. Surely they will turn away your hearts after their gods." Solomon clung to these in love. And he had seven hundred wives, princesses, and three hundred concubines; and his wives turned away his heart. For it was so, when Solomon was old, that his*

wives turned his heart after other gods; and his heart was not loyal to the Lord his God, as was the heart of his father David." (1 Kings 11:1-4)

In the preceding chapters of 1 Kings, we read of the exploits of Solomon, of great military triumphs, the building of the temple, his personal palace, and ridiculous wealth. When the Queen of Sheba came to visit, she declared after observing all Solomon's wealth, "the half was not told me" (1 Kings 10:7).

The eleventh chapter begins with "*but.*" *But* is a conjunction. A conjunction is a word used to connect words, phrases, clauses, or sentences. As such, it ties two things together. "But" as used in our text, links Solomon's success: his riches, fame, and fortune with his failure.

Each of us can speak of God's divine providence at some level. He has blessed us all in some way or another. Often times we speak of others who have received an extravagant blessing and after speaking of what they have received we will add a conjunction. We might say, "You know he has this or that," and then add the conjunction, "but, he has cancer." "You know he has this or that," or, "he has become this or that," and add the conjunction, "but he and his wife do not get along," "but their child is in jail," or, "but he or she is not very smart." In spite of all that a person has, all that they may be or have done, a conjunction somehow serves to bring balance. A conjunction can serve to connect our:

- Blessings with our shortcomings
- Successes with our failures

- Strengths with our frailties
- Potential with our reality
- Past to our present
- Present to our future

Solomon had one weakness, one little weakness in the midst of all these strengths. However, it was to be his undoing. It started small, like many disasters. He married an Egyptian princess, it seemed to be OK in that she gave up her idols and false gods, and worshiped the true God, the God of Israel. Then he decided that he wanted more than one wife. Therefore, he took a second wife. Then he decided that he wanted someone else, so he took a third. Then he wanted a harem, like the kings of the surrounding nations. *The lust of the flesh, the lust of the eyes, and the pride of life* (1 John 2:16) would be his downfall. Solomon's compromise, his conjunction, snowballed from one indulgence to a blizzard of many.

We wonder why a man with such great wisdom might do so. Maybe we find reason in the words of the poet James Weldon Johnson as he wrote of The Prodigal Son (God's Trombones, 1955),

"Oh, the women of Babylon!
Dressed in yellow and purple and scarlet,
Loaded with rings and earrings and bracelets,
Their lips like a honeycomb dripping with honey,
Perfumed and sweet-smelling like a jasmine flower;
And the jasmine smell of the Babylon women
Got in his nostrils and went to his head,"

Solomon started to make alliances with other kings, and married their daughters. He took concubines (women he lived with or was intimate with without being married to—second class wives, if you will) from other nations, forgetting that Israel was God's special people set apart to worship him alone. Some of these women worshipped the Lord, but others stuck to their own religions and their idols. The king of Israel should not have allowed this. He had no right to allow the Promised Land to be polluted by false worship. However, he did not want to upset his wives, so he ignored it, and one compromise led to another. He then allowed them to worship openly. Why make his wives hide away what they were doing? Surely, it was better to be open!

The next compromise was to facilitate their worship. In order to be happy, Solomon's wives needed to be able to sacrifice. They needed priests and ceremonial robes. Keep in mind Solomon was rich; he could afford it. He built temples and idols for them. It was not as if he would worship them himself or make anyone else do so.

Next, he started to worship alongside them taking part in their rites and rituals. What did it matter? He was still sacrificing to the Lord! Besides, all religions are basically the same, aren't they?

Solomon's conjunction, Solomon's downfall was that with all his wisdom he failed to follow the wisdom of God. God had commanded and warned, *"You shall not intermarry with them, nor they with you. Surely they will turn away your hearts after their gods."* Gradual compromise had led him to a place where the greatest king in Israel's history was living in open rebellion and disobedience to the God who had given him everything.

We are all affected by some conjunction in our lives. No matter what our age or stage in life may be; we have a conjunction. We have a thorn or a thistle. Something of what we could say, "but for this" or "but for that" everything would be all right. Each of us could say, "But for my husband, my significant other, but for my wife, but for my job, but for my credit card bills everything would be all right." Growing in spiritual knowledge and God's grace is about either getting our conjunction changed, healed, or learning to live with whatever it is in a positive manner.

If you do not know Jesus Christ as Lord and Savior, there is a conjunction in your life. No matter how much you may have. No matter how great your job, fine your car, or big your house. No matter what people may think of you and about you, if you do not know Jesus you have a conjunction. You have the disease of sin, and the cleansing blood of Jesus Christ is the only thing that can heal that disease. Jesus is the divine conjunction that separates your past from your present. He is the conjunction that separates you from being sinner or saint. Jesus is the divine conjunction.

When we follow our own wisdom, or the wisdom of men, we cannot help but to end in disaster. We may have all the things and stuff that life offers, but fail in that which truly matters, our relationship with God.

IS SOLOMON'S ADVICE CREDIBLE?

"My son, hear the instruction of your father, and do not forsake the law of your mother; . . ." (Proverbs 1:8)

The Proverbs were originally designed to constitute a teaching manual for young men and it is generally believed that these were men being trained to administer the affairs of the empire of Solomon. Learning is for the young and inexperienced but not for them only. One who has already experienced much and who is naturally perceptive can continue learning by means of the wisdom that these proverbs offer.

The book of Proverbs is a book of instruction. Much of what Solomon has to say is related to relationships. Knowing his history, one may think "who better" or "who better not" to give advice. What are we to make of his wisdom regarding relationships?

Solomon's writings at times seem to approve monogamy, lifelong faithfulness to one wife. He wrote in Proverbs 5:18, 19,

"Let your fountain be blessed, and rejoice with the wife of your youth. As a loving deer and a graceful doe, let her breasts satisfy you at all times; and always be enraptured with her love."

He wrote in Ecclesiastes 9:9,

"Live joyfully with the wife whom you love all the days of your vain life which He has given you

under the sun, all your days of vanity; for that is your portion in life, and in the labor which you perform under the sun."

However, Solomon also wrote in Proverbs 18:22, *"He who finds a wife finds a good thing"* and it seems that he himself found one as often as possible.

Solomon was amazing; he was one of the wisest, the richest, and the most powerful men in the world, all at the same time. He seemingly had it all, but there was one thing that changed everything, he did what God told him not to do. Unfortunately, Solomon made a book of proverbs, but a book of proverbs never made a Solomon. However, his weaknesses, shortcomings, and conjunctions did not totally disqualify him from being a wise man.

What then are we to make of the declaration of Solomon's wisdom? We can probably assume that these proverbs were written out of Solomon's life experience, some during better days, and some during worse. We can assume that these are the sum of his life experience and not the outcome of any one-day, week, etc.

I would like to think that when God looks at our lives, the good days will outweigh the bad. The wise days will outweigh the foolish, and that our wisdom or lack thereof will not be judged by any age or stage, but that God would look from beginning to end and based on the total, say, *"Well done, good and faithful servant"* (Matt. 25:21).

When using those criteria we can find that yes, Solomon's advice is credible. There may be inconsistencies between his life and his life lessons, but he still has good advice to share.

A youngster brought home a report card heavy with poor grades. His mother asked, "What have you to say about this?" The boy replied, "One thing is for sure, you know I ain't cheating!"

If God were to look at the totality of your life experience what would be his finding? What would he have you to say about the life you have lived? It will not be perfect, but whatever it is it must be the truth.

Whatever we read and see of Solomon, the good, bad, and the ugly it was his own. In spite of all the wealth, wisdom, and riches he had a void in his life. As much as he tried, neither women nor riches could fill his emptiness. He was happy with what he had, but he missed out on happiness.

When we stand before God, we will have to give an account of the life that we lived. We will not be able to use the excuse that we cheated, that we copied someone else's life. Whatever we are, the good, the bad, or the ugly, it will be our own.

I do not know about you, but I am thankful that God does not look at each day, week, or month of my life, but looks from beginning to end, taking the totality of my life into account. My hope and prayer is that the end is better than the beginning. That somehow during the in-between, I have been able to eliminate some of the conjunctions in my life.

REFLECTIONS AND MEDITATIONS

1. On what basis do you establish the creditability of the advice you receive?
2. What is the conjunction (and, but, or) in your life?
3. Are there life lessons you have learned that have not been applied to your life?
4. What subtle compromises can you identify that, like termites, are eating away at your obedience to God's Word?
5. Have you marked your bible without your bible marking you?

PRAYER

Thank God that your spiritual creditability is not based on your daily performance, but on your eternal position in Jesus Christ.

Chapter 2

WHO'S LOOKING?

If you choose to remain single, recognize that you can enjoy all the benefits of a marital relationship, with the exception of sex.

"He who finds a wife . . ." *(Proverbs 18:22)*

A short statement was written by a young woman entitled, *How To Stop People From Bugging You About Getting Married.* She writes; old aunts used to come up to me at weddings, poking me in the ribs and cackling, telling me, "You're next." They stopped after I started doing the same thing to them at funerals.

Solomon presupposes in this verse that everyone desires to be married, that marriage is a good thing, particularly to the right woman, and that in the relationship favor with God is found. In reality, not everyone is called to, or desires to be married. Jesus spoke of this reality in Matthew 19:12,

> *"For there are eunuchs who were born thus from their mother's womb, and there are eunuchs who were made eunuchs by men, and there are eunuchs who have made themselves eunuchs for the kingdom of heaven's sake. He, who is able to accept it, let him accept it."*

The International Children's Bible states it ever so simply this way,

> *"There are different reasons why some men cannot marry. Some men were born without the ability to become fathers. Others were made that way later in life by other people. And other men have given up marriage because of the kingdom of heaven. But the person who can marry should accept this teaching about marriage."*

Apparently, not everyone can accept these sayings. Jesus said those who can should not bind themselves by a vow that they will never marry only that in the mind they are now in, they purpose not to marry. Those who can accept this should accept it.

Some men have attained a holy lack of interest to all the delights of the married state. They have determined the increase of God's grace is better than the increase of the family, and fellowship with the

Father and with His Son Jesus Christ is to be preferred before any other fellowship.

Admittedly, those who do not marry for spiritual reasons are few in number, but they do exist. However, for the great majority of men there are no such limitations to marriage. Solomon believed in marriage, having over 700 wives, but he seemingly did not believe in monogamy-one man joined to one woman for life.

In our modern society, where people believe in freedom of expression, and opportunities abound, particularly in the sexual arena, we ask the question, who's looking to get married? Whether you are looking or not, there are some things that you as a single need to understand.

THE CRITERIA FOR LIVING SINGLE

> *"But I say to the unmarried and to the widows: It is good for them if they remain even as I am; but if they cannot exercise self-control, let them marry. For it is better to marry than to burn with passion." (1 Corinthians 7:8-9)*

One bitterly cold winter night a young man plodded through knee-high snow to the home of the girl he had been dating regularly. Tonight was the night. He asked her to marry him. Being very practical, the young woman replied, "When you have several thousand dollars, I will seriously consider it." Six months later, the two strolled hand in hand through a park along the river. He stopped to kiss her and asked, "When are we going to get married?" She inquired, "Well, you remember my condition.

Just how much money have you saved?" He responded, "Exactly seventy-five dollars." She sighed and smiled, "Oh well, I guess that's close enough!"

Just as this woman had criteria for the transition from being single to being married, God has criteria as well. Unlike the young woman, and contrary to what many think in our society, God is not willing to compromise or settle for less.

Not everyone is called to be married. There are some God has called to live the single life. Whether you feel called of God, or have chosen of your own accord to remain single, there are certain criteria that God has established. Some desire to have the best of both worlds; the freedom of being single and the security and sexual convenience of being married. However, you cannot have the best of both worlds and be obedient to God. Yes, you can find companionship, good intellectual conversation, a partner for activities, etc., but God has limited the relationships you are to have with the opposite sex, not to include sex.

With the ratio of women to men being in some places sixteen to one, that does not mean that you can violate God's commandment more often. It simply means there is a greater selection, a greater opportunity for men to find that good woman. Unfortunately, there is also a greater opportunity for men and women to compromise. However, regardless of the greater opportunities, God has a standard.

1 Corinthians 6:18-20 (NIV) tells us,

> *"Flee from sexual immorality. All other sins a man commits are outside his body, but he who sins*

sexually sins against his own body. Do you not know that your body is a temple of the Holy Spirit, who is in you, whom you have received from God? You are not your own; you were bought at a price. Therefore honor God with your body."

If you are one who is not looking to get married, if you are one who wants to but has not met your significant other, you have only one choice sexually—abstinence. There are no other options for you to remain single within the will of God and experience his favor. Author C. S. Lewis said, "There is no getting away from it: the old Christian rule is either marriage, with complete faithfulness to your partner, or else total abstinence." The reality however is chastity, sexual purity, is the most unpopular of our Christian virtues.

A beautiful woman shares: "When we date, we start giving gifts, like flowers or candy. When a couple becomes engaged, they give special things—a diamond and very personal things. The most personal gift that I can ever give is myself. I have nothing more precious to give. When I marry, I want to give my husband the best that I have—my whole self as completely as I can."

Young man, young woman, if you want to obtain God's favor you will have to do it God's way. If you choose to remain single, recognize that you can enjoy all the benefits of a relationship outside of sex. The sexual relationship is reserved for the marriage bed. You cannot and must not setup and play house.

If you are unable to restrain your sexual yearnings and passion, Paul says that you ought to be looking to marry rather than remain single and be consumed with lust.

MEN HAVE A DESIRE FOR A MATE

> *"So Adam gave names to all cattle, to the birds of the air, and to every beast of the field. But for Adam there was not found a helper comparable to him. And the Lord God caused a deep sleep to fall on Adam, and he slept; and He took one of his ribs, and closed up the flesh in its place. Then the rib which the Lord God had taken from man He made into a woman, and He brought her to the man. And Adam said: "This is now bone of my bones and flesh of my flesh; she shall be called Woman, because she was taken out of Man." Therefore a man shall leave his father and mother and be joined to his wife, and they shall become one flesh." (Genesis 2:20-24)*

From the beginning, man has had a missing element. Adam, after naming all the animals of the earth recognized that there was something missing. This was the chief reason for God assembling the creatures. It was meant to reveal his loneliness. The longing for a partner was already deeply seated in his nature, and the survey of the animals, coming to him probably in pairs, could not fail but to intensify that secret hunger of his soul. Every animal had someone; but Adam had no one like himself. Whether he knew it or not, Adam needed and was looking for someone like himself.

To satisfy his need God performed surgery, took a rib, and used it to create a woman, a helpmate for the man. The woman was not taken from man's head to rule over him or from his foot to be downtrodden. She was taken from and area next to his heart to be loved, cherished, and to be his helper, a companion to walk by his side in all of life's experiences.

When God brought Eve to Adam, he joined them in a marital relationship saying, *"Therefore a man shall leave his father and mother and be joined to his wife, and they shall become one flesh"* (Genesis 2:24). By God's decree, the man is to take the initiative to leave his father and mother and be joined to his wife. The man is to be the catalyst in the forming of the marital relationship.

Some women and men have their roles confused. Women are now the seekers and men are the ones found. Women are the pursuers and men are the pursued.

My brothers, whether single or married, God has placed in you the need for companionship for the opposite sex. There is no way that you can honestly say that you do not need her.

WOMEN HAVE A DESIRE FOR A MATE

> *"To the woman He said: "I will greatly multiply your sorrow and your conception; in pain you shall bring forth children; your desire shall be for your husband, and he shall rule over you." (Genesis 3:16)*

It is questionable whether the second half of this verse, *"your desire shall be for your husband, and he shall rule over you"* speaks of sexual desire in women, or whether it alludes to her natural desire for children.

The curse of Genesis 3:16, resultant of the sin of Adam and Eve in the Garden of Eden, is not a popular one, nor one that would be politically correct in our day and time, but is nonetheless to some extent true. Whether married or single from the time when God gave Eve to Adam, there is a natural desire for women towards men.

In their desire for companionship, the questions on many women's mind are: "How can I make this person love me?" "What can I do to get him to notice me?" In a competitive world where meaningful relationships are at a premium, the following advice would seem prudent.

First, make sure that you are looking for a godly man. The bible says you ought to be equally yoked. Then, you must hold up your standard. If you want a godly man, you must be a godly woman. Men do not respect you more when you compromise your integrity. Do not dumb down who you are. Women you may not want to hear this, but the reason there are fewer good men is because they have been given too many options to be financially irresponsible and to fulfill their sexual fantasies without any commitment.

Second, realize that you are already a whole person. Yes, marriage can be fulfilling, and rewarding, but it is not the *be* all and *end* all of life. Self-development ought to be your first priority. You ought to educate yourself, beautify yourself for yourself, and achieve as much financial success as you can by yourself. Be the person you desire to be and become happy and sufficient within yourself. It is only then that you will have something of significance to share with someone else. Men will tend to take advantage of a needy woman, but are also often reluctant with a self-sufficient woman who declares she does not need any man. Somewhere in the middle is the woman you need to be.

Third, do not start with a substitute. Some women who are married, married substitutes, they married someone who maybe looked like the real thing, or they wanted to believe he was the real thing only to find out differently later. If you want him to be a Christian, do not accept little glimmers of morality and spirituality as substitutes for a commitment to Christ. If you want him to be a responsible husband and provider, do not accept him taking you to the movies and out to dinner where you go dutch. Some women reason that at least you did not have to pay for both, and in a marriage, everything is 50-50, or that you did not want to be committed to him in any way. However, if a man cannot afford to pay for movie and a dinner now, it is a good sign he cannot pay the house note. If he is working every day and does not have a car, and you have to go and pick him up, it is a good indication that he is missing something in his management skills. Bottom line: Do not think him, wish him, or hope him, into being something that he is not. Do not start with a substitute.

Fourth, do not compromise biblical guidelines. Too many women are compromising their spiritual integrity in the hopes that the satisfaction of sexual need will cause some man to love them. If you truly want to find love let him live in his own apartment or house and you live in yours. Convenience and financial arrangements are no basis to compromise your spiritual integrity. It slaps God in the face to say that you have to live with someone to make it financially. If that is the case, why not get a female roommate instead of a male. It speaks of the fact that you are trusting in the ways of the world more than you are trusting in God.

Whether single or married, God has placed in you the need for companionship from the opposite sex; therefore, you ought to be looking. But make sure that you do not compromise who you are.

A humorous story is told of a "Husband Shopping Center" that opened in Dallas, where women could go to choose a husband from among many men. It was laid out in five floors, with the men increasing in positive attributes as you ascended the floors. The only rule was, once you opened the door to any floor, you must choose a man from that floor, and if you went up a floor, you could not go back down except to leave the place never to return.

A couple of girlfriends went to the place to find men. First floor, the door had a sign saying, "These men have jobs and love kids." The women read the sign and said, "Well, that's better than not having jobs, or not loving kids, but I wonder what's further up?" So up they went.

Second floor says, "These men have high paying jobs, love kids, and are extremely good looking." Hmmm, say the women. But, I wonder what's further up?

Third floor, "These men have high paying jobs, are extremely good looking, love kids and help with the housework." Wow! Said the women. Very tempting, but, there's more further up! And up they went.

Fourth floor, "These men have high paying jobs, love kids, are extremely good looking, help with the housework, and have a strong romantic streak." Oh, mercy me, said one woman. But just think! What might be awaiting us further on!

So up to the fifth floor they go. The sign on that door said, "This floor is empty and exists only to prove that women are impossible to please. Good-bye."

What is said of these women is also true of men; both men and women are looking for companionship, and both seem impossible to please. Whether we are talking about women or men, both need to have realistic expectations.

As I previously stated, men and women, if you want to obtain God's favor you will have to do it God's way. If you choose to remain single, recognize that you can enjoy all the benefits of a relationship outside of sex. The sexual relationship is reserved for the marriage bed. You cannot and must not setup and play house. If you cannot contain, you ought to be looking. The Apostle Paul's advice is that *"it is better to marry than to burn with passion"* (1 Corinthians 7:9).

If you are looking for real love, sincere love, committed love, John 3:16 declares, *"For God so loved the world that He gave His only begotten Son, that whoever believes in Him should not perish but have everlasting life."* You may not have found the perfect man, the perfect woman, but you can find the perfect Savior. God loves you, and he loves you now. You never have to worry if he loves you. God's love is not a love that can be bought, enticed, or entrapped. He loves you with a love that knows no bounds. He wants to be your inspiration, encouragement, enlightenment, confidant, intercessor, lover, and your Savior.

REFLECTIONS AND MEDITATIONS

1. How do you respond emotionally and intellectually to the supposition that not everyone is called to be married?
2. What has been the greatest challenge for you as a single?
3. What biblical criteria have you established for consideration of a mate?
4. How realistic are your expectations in considering a mate?

PRAYER

Ask God to keep you from compromise as you experience the natural yearnings towards finding a mate. Ask him to help you experience personal growth and spiritual maturity in your time of waiting.

Chapter 3

WHAT DOES A GOOD THING LOOK LIKE?

If you are looking for a mate, make yourself a good thing, throw yourself in the lost and found, and wait to be found by someone who recognizes a treasure when they see it.

"He who finds a wife finds a good thing, . . ." (Proverbs 18:22)

Have you ever made New Year's resolutions? Maybe it was to lose weight, pay down your credit cards, or go back to school. Maybe you were one who said, that you would meet someone new. If so, do you remember either the mental or the written list of steps you would take to make it happen? Typically, after a month has gone by, like most people's resolutions, they are but distant memories.

Solomon says, *"He who finds a wife finds a good thing, and obtains favor from the Lord."* If you are looking for a godly mate to marry and raise a family, or just looking for that special person to spend some quality time with, you need to keep our scripture text foremost in your mind throughout your "courting days"! Everyone whether their intentions are towards marriage or not, is looking for a good thing, looking for that special person who fits all, or at least most of their guidelines—but, still a good thing. That being true, what does a good thing look like? Good things are obviously of both genders, men and women, but because Solomon's emphasis is on the woman, we will give her our attention.

WHAT DOES A GOOD THING LOOK LIKE?

Most of us men have in our head the image of a good thing, the ideal woman. Some men might say the ideal woman is a woman who will obey (now there's a nasty word) their every whim, wait on them hand and foot, and literally worship the ground they walk on (I think the word for this is male chauvinism, or in a simpler word "crazy").

On the other hand, some women have in their minds a different image. Some say the ideal woman can do the work of two men, and if women were prime ministers and presidents, wars would end, unemployment would be eliminated, and world hunger would be a thing of the past. (I think the word for this is extreme feminism, or in a simpler word "crazy"). Both men and women have some crazy images in their heads. The reality of what the ideal woman looks like lies somewhere between these two extremes.

What is the “ideal woman” like? Liz Higgs says, "The ideal woman was described 2,500 years ago in Proverbs 31—and she is still intimidating her sisters ever since." Proverbs 31 describes the virtuous woman: the ideal woman, wife, and mother.

When we examine this ancient biblical ideal of womanhood, we do not find the stereotypical homemaker occupied with dirty dishes and laundry, her daily life dictated by the demands of her husband and her children. Nor do we find a hardened, overly ambitious career woman who leaves her family to fend for itself. What we find is a strong, dignified, multitalented, caring woman who is an individual in her own right. This woman has money to invest, servants to look after and real estate to manage. She is her husband’s partner, and she is completely trusted with the responsibility for their lands, property, and goods. She has the business skills to buy and sell in the market, along with the heartfelt sensitivity and compassion to care for and fulfill the needs of people who are less fortunate. Cheerfully and energetically, she tackles the challenges each day brings. Her husband and children love and respect her for her kind, generous and caring nature. The virtuous woman is an example, I believe, of what Almighty God intended when he created "Eve" to walk alongside and with the first Adam as a helpmate. Maya Angelo would say that she is a “phenomenal woman.”

However, with all her responsibilities, first, she looks to God. Her primary concern is God’s will in her life. What does a good thing look like? She is a woman after God's own heart. Proverbs 30:30 (NIV) declares, *"Charm is deceptive, and beauty is fleeting; but a woman who fears the LORD is to be praised."* No matter what other attributes the ideal woman might have physically, mentally, educationally, she is first spiritually connected to her God.

YOU NEED TO HAVE REALISTIC EXPECTATIONS

In the previous chapter, we determined that if you, as a single person, cannot contain, that is, are in danger of being consumed by your lust and compromise of biblical standards you need to be looking. Again, Paul says of the unmarried and widows, *"if they cannot exercise self-control, let them marry. For it is better to marry than to burn with passion"* (1 Corinthians 7:8-9). If that describes you, you ought to be looking.

> *"Marriage should be honored by all, and the marriage bed kept pure, for God will judge the adulterer and all the sexually immoral." (Hebrews 13:4, NIV)*

> *"Do you not know that the wicked will not inherit the kingdom of God? Do not be deceived: Neither the sexually immoral nor idolaters nor adulterers nor male prostitutes nor homosexual offenders nor thieves nor the greedy nor drunkards nor slanderers nor swindlers will inherit the kingdom of God." (1 Corinthians 6:9-10, NIV)*

That being true, what criteria do you use to determine a good thing? The venue for finding a good thing is dating, going together, hangin' out together, whatever you may want to call it.

Many people misunderstand the purpose of dating. Dating ought to help you determine and get settled in your mind what attributes you are looking for in a person: personality, communication skills, sincerity, sensitivity, etc. Dating is not intended to be the venue for your sexual fulfillment. It is intended for you to get to know the other person. Falling in love ought to be a byproduct of your determination that you and that person are compatible in as many areas as possible.

Relationships are in some ways like fruit (recognizably all analogies break down at some point—so do not take this farther than I am taking it). When we go to the grocery store, we want the unbruised apple, the firm orange, the yellow banana, and firm but not to firm pears and peaches. We do not want that which is spoiled, or on its way to being spoiled. Some people expect that every piece of fruit is going to be firm, sweet, and satisfying. The reality is that neither fruit, nor life, is that way. The reality is that most of us have been bumped, bruised, and scarred. However, just because we have some bad spots does not disqualify us from being useful, eligible, and able to live happily ever after. In fact, our bruises may qualify us for some things. If you are making banana bread, you do not want firm bananas, you want some of those that are softer and bruised a bit. Experience is a most desirable asset if it has led to maturity. Because a person has been bruised in life does not make them unusable or undesirable. Some people sweeten as they mature, as they grow older. Some on the other hand, dwell on their defects, bumps, bruises, scars and rot.

The fact is that we all have defects. Some of us see our defects as major, while others see them as minor and the opposite is true as well. Some of us see our defects as minor and others see them as major. As with anything, there are compromises. You probably heard about the newlyweds. On their honeymoon, the groom took his bride by the hand and said, "Now that we're married, dear, I hope you won't mind if I mention a few little defects that I've noticed about you." "Not at all," the bride replied with a deceptive sweetness. "It was those little defects that kept me from getting a better husband."

In reality, our relationships are more like watermelons: all different shapes, sizes, shades, markings, but yet similar on the outside and about the same firmness. It is hard to tell what a watermelon tastes like on the inside. They are costly and once home too big and messy to return. We can never know how sweet it is until we get it home and open it up. In relationships, we never really come to know a person until some circumstance cuts them open and allows us to see who they really are. Moreover, by that time, the relationship may have become too big, entangled, and messy to return to where we were. That's why you need to give relationships time to mature, such that, you may see all that you can before you make a commitment, before you get romantically and surely, before you get sexually involved.

Dating like the picking of fruit ought to be done cautiously with the end in mind. Depending upon your goals, you ought not to go out with some people. When it comes to a good thing, for the Christian, some things are non-negotiable. As a Christian, you ought not to consider a serious relationship with someone who is not saved. I do not mean someone who is a churchgoer, but one who is truly committed to the Lord.

YOU MAY NEED TO RENEW YOUR GOOD THING

The following letter appeared in the syndicated advice column of the Chicago Sun-Times addressed to columnist Ann Landers. For about 45 years, the column was a regular feature in many newspapers across North America.

Dear Ann Landers:

I am a 21-year-old girl who was dating a great guy. He is 27, sophisticated, fun to be with, and I felt so lucky to be going out with him. He invited me to go to San Francisco for the weekend. I couldn't get off work and felt awful about it. He said, "I'll bring you back something nice." Well, what he brought back was herpes. I am so furious I feel like screaming. Of course, I have stopped seeing him, but I am afraid to go out with anyone else. I would rather die than give somebody what that "great guy" gave me. A really sweet fellow who works in this office has asked me out, but I'm scared to get involved. My whole life seems wrecked. I'm angry and depressed and feel as if I'm not worthy of a decent man. I know this is a terrible attitude for a 21-year-old. Can you help me?—*Typhoid Mary in Amarillo, TX.*

You may be living with the regret of some relationship. It may be more or less serious than this woman's. Your past may be emotionally taxing you to the point of periodic depression, sleeplessness, loneliness, or a host of other regrets. However, no matter what your past looks like you do not have to wallow in it.

If you have messed up, compromised, or been disobedient, you need to know that you cannot go back, but you can go on. The consequences will not go away, your children will still be your children, your STD will still be your STD, your bills will still be your bills, and your scars your scars. However, in God's sight you can go forward to experience forgiveness, grace, and mercy with a clean heart, a renewed mind, and a renewed spirit.

David's repentant response to his adulterous relationship with Bathsheba was, *"Create in me a clean heart, O God, and renew a steadfast spirit within me."* (Psalm 51:10)

As said earlier, if you are looking for a mate, make yourself a good thing, throw yourself in the lost and found, and wait to be found by someone who recognizes a treasure when they see it. You may think of yourself as having no value or worth, but someone out there does.

How do you make yourself a good thing? Acknowledge what you are spiritually.

"If we say that we have no sin, we deceive ourselves, and the truth is not in us. If we confess our sins, He is faithful and just to forgive us our sins and to cleanse us from all unrighteousness." (1 John 1:8-9)

If you have compromised in the area of your sexuality, there is such a thing as second virginity, spiritual renewal:

"Therefore, if anyone is in Christ, he is a new creation; old things have passed away; behold, all things have become new." (2 Corinthians 5:17)

God will give you grace to understand that no one is perfect in a real world, to understand that you are not alone. Many others are in the same position. Whatever you have experienced is not unique.

"No temptation has overtaken you except such as is common to man." (1 Corinthians 10:13)

God will give you mercy to deal with the broken heart or broken home. Help you to deal with the wayward child, and with all the heartaches of decades of mothering.

"My grace is sufficient for you, for My strength is made perfect in weakness." (2 Corinthians 12:9)

I'm not excusing inappropriate behavior; I am saying there is a God to help you through.

Regardless of your situation, you need to know that God understands.

> *"For this reason he had to be made like his brothers in every way, in order that he might become a merciful and faithful high priest in service to God, and that he might make atonement for the sins of the people. Because he himself suffered when he was tempted, he is able to help those who are being tempted. " (Hebrews 2:17-18, NIV)*

Christ understands what it is like to live in the real world. He deals with us where we are. God loves you. No matter what your past may look like, you can go on from this moment in the fullness of His might. You cannot go back, but you can go on. You can be renewed and become God's good thing.

What does a good thing look like? The model woman described in Proverbs is a portrait of ideal womanhood. Her Godly characteristics can be applied to all women: single, married, divorced, and widowed. Cultures change, styles change, traditions become outdated, and technology advances, but a godly woman, a good thing, keeps God as her focus, and realizes that regardless of her natural talents, acquired skills, or all her accomplishments, her strength comes from God. A good thing puts God first and desires to do His will.

"Who can find a good thing?" Make sure your expectations are realistic. Beauty to some extent is in the eye of the beholder. Some of us think the grass is always greener on the other side of the fence. Accepting the defects in others, and learning to love and appreciate those defects is what sincere, loving, and genuine relationships are all about. A 10 year-old boy was asked, "How would you make a marriage work?" He replied, "Tell your wife she looks pretty even if she looks like a truck."

Do you need to become a good thing? If you have made some mistakes, been bumped, bruised, and scarred know that God loves you. He is a God of love, forgiveness, mercy, grace, and renewal. If you make a commitment to change, you can be assured that you will have God's help to become a good thing. You cannot go back, but you can go on.

REFLECTIONS AND MEDITATIONS

1. What is your mental image of what a "good thing" looks like? Does it line up with Scripture?
2. What is your purpose in dating?
3. Have you asked God for and received forgiveness and cleansing for past sins? Have you forgiven yourself?
4. Have you experienced spiritual renewal and how has it daily being manifested in your life?

PRAYER

Ask God for spiritual renewal from your past; and to give you a mind to go on with a sense of dignity, joy, and peace.

Chapter 4

OBTAINING GOD'S FAVOR

We do not normally think of relationships as engendering God's favor.

"He who finds a wife finds a good thing, and obtains favor from the Lord." (Proverbs 18:22)

I believe we sometimes overemphasize the matter of salvation. We stress that the most important thing is to be saved. Although that is certainly true, a personal relationship with God that opens the door to our salvation is just the beginning. When we enter through the door of salvation, an abundance of blessings awaits us. Matthew 6:33 declares, *"But seek first his kingdom and his righteousness, and all these things will be given to you as well."* It is the *"all these things shall be given to you as well"* that should be our concern. All *these things* are God's blessings that are showered on us because of God's favor. Many of us have grasped God's salvation, but are missing His favor. As we think about this matter of obtaining God's favor, Solomon clearly says that by the act of a man finding a wife (a good thing) and entering into a marital relationship, favor is obtained from the Lord. In so saying, Solomon seems to be saying that favor is something that can be desired, pursued, and found. If so, what kinds of things can we do, or what are the ways to pursue God's favor? What can we do, must we do, to be blessed of God? How can we obtain God's favor? To understand this matter we must first understand . . .

THE DISTINCTION BETWEEN FAVOR AND GRACE

The word favor is found many more times in the Old Testament than in the New Testament (64 OT; 6 NT). The Hebrew word most used is *Khane*, and literally means grace, charm, acceptance, goodwill, or desire. As used in our text it is *raw-tsone'*, which means acceptable, delight, desire, favor, or good pleasure.

As we see, one of the descriptive terms of favor is grace. Grace, unlike favor, is found extensively throughout the New Testament (37 OT; 122 NT). The Greek word for grace is *Kharis*, meaning (1) the forgiveness and mercy of God, (2) the blessings of enjoyment of God's favor.

Because we find the word grace in the description of favor, and favor in the description of grace, there are those who say that God's grace and God's favor are the same. However, they are not the same. In fact, grace and favor are quite different. Grace is a free gift; favor may be deserved or gained.

WHAT IS GRACE?

The traditional definition of grace is as follows: Grace is the unmerited, undeserved, and unearned favor of God. Grace is something that cannot be obtained by any meritorious act. You do not deserve it because of birthright, social, political, or any other status, and there is nothing that you can do to earn it. It is something God gives to you.

Ephesians 2:8, 9 declares, *"For by grace you have been saved through faith, and that not of yourselves; it is the gift of God, not of works, lest anyone should boast."* Although it is through faith, we come to believe. It is God's grace, extended to all of humanity, which allows us even to consider the matter of being saved. Had not God by grace first extended this opportunity to come, had not God first beckoned us to himself, there would be no way that sinful humanity could dare approach the throne of God.

In Christ, we have received grace. John 1:12 declares,

> *"But as many as received Him, to them He gave the right to become children of God, to those who believe in His name."*

John 1:16-17 declares,

> *"And of His fullness we have all received, and grace for grace. For the law was given through*

Moses, but grace and truth came through Jesus Christ"

All true believers receive from Christ's fullness; the best and greatest saints cannot live without him, the meanest and weakest may live by him. Let us see what we have received.

We have received *grace for grace*, meaning that God gave extended grace *to* us in Jesus Christ, but he did not stop there, he continues to extend grace *in* us through Jesus Christ. Christ is both the source of God's grace *to* us and the source of grace continuing *in* us. As the

- Reservoir receives water from the fullness of the flowing fountain
- Branches, sap from the fullness of the root
- Air, light from the fullness of the sun

So, we receive *grace* for salvation and *grace* to live abundantly everyday from the fullness of Christ. We have received *grace for grace.*

WHAT IS GOD'S FAVOR?

Grace is the unmerited, undeserved, and unearned gift of God. Favor, on the other hand, is obtainable through meritorious deeds. Scripture affirms that we can obtain God's favor.

Let not mercy and truth forsake you; bind them around your neck, write them on the tablet of your heart, and so find favor and high esteem in the sight of God and man. (Proverbs 3:3-4)

> *He who earnestly seeks good finds favor, but trouble will come to him who seeks evil. (Proverbs 11:27)*

> *A good man obtains favor from the Lord, but a man of wicked intentions He will condemn. (Proverbs 12:2)*

When we think about the fact of whether or not favor can be obtained, we have to turn to the hallmark verse of Luke 2:52 which declares, *"And Jesus increased in wisdom and stature, and in favor with God and men."* As Jesus grew up and matured he increased in favor with God and man, that is, in all those qualities that rendered him acceptable to God and man that are illuminated in Galatians 5:22-23, *"But the fruit of the Spirit is love, joy, peace, longsuffering, kindness, goodness, faithfulness, gentleness, self-control."* The image of God shone brighter in him as a man, than it did, or could, while he was an infant and a child. As we exercise the fruit of the Spirit, we grow in favor.

As we grow in physical stature, we should also grow in wisdom; consequently, as we grow in wisdom, we will grow in favor with God and man. As we mature as Christians, we can increase and obtain more favor with God. As the manifestation of the fruit of the Spirit is released in us, and through us, we ought to experience more of God's favor.

When we attend Bible study, Sunday school, prayer meeting, or exercise our personal disciplines of prayer, bible reading, and fellowship, it ought to be with the mind of increasing in *wisdom and stature*, and *in favor* with God and men. Favor comes as we spend time with God. Favor comes to those who do what is right!

Do not fall into the trap that favor is just about God blessing us with money. Favor doesn't always translate into riches! Proverbs 22:1 declares, *"A good name is to be more desired than great riches, favor is better than silver and gold."* Look at the verse again, a good name is more desired. Besides, some with little money have a much greater favor than those who have great wealth: James 2:5 declares,

> *"Listen, my beloved brethren: did not God choose the poor of this world to be rich in faith and heirs of the kingdom which He promised to those who love Him?"*

Favor is the special affection of God toward you that releases an influence on you, so that others are inclined to like you or to cooperate with you whether they like you or not! In other words, God really likes you!

ARE YOU MISSING GOD'S FAVOR?

Some men have found a good thing, married her, but are not experiencing the fullness of God's favor. The reason some of us are not receiving God's favor is because we are not growing up and maturing in Christ. (I've lived long enough to know that many folks look saved whose houses are messed up!) If we want to see more of God's favor released in our homes, on our jobs, in our marriages, and generally, in our lives, we have to seek to grow up and mature in him. In order to mature in him, we must apply biblical standards to our relationships.

The wrong attitude of husbands toward wives can cause result in missing God's favor. Scripture informs us:

> *Husbands, likewise, dwell with them with understanding, giving honor to the wife, as to the weaker vessel, and as being heirs together of the grace of life, that your prayers may not be hindered. (1 Peter 3:7)*

Strife, pulling against each other, instead of pulling together, in the household can cause us to miss God's favor

> *Giving thanks always for all things to God the Father in the name of our Lord Jesus Christ, submitting to one another in the fear of God. (Ephesians 5:20-21)*

A relationship not established on the right foundation can cause us to miss God's favor. Some of us lived together before you were married and never repented of that sin, never asked God for forgiveness. You need to repent if you want God's favor.

Disobedience can cause you to miss God's favor. Some are more concerned about personal and sexual satisfaction than God's favor; too many are looking for the good thing, but not for God's favor.

When husband and wives cannot get along, it causes God grief. When you fail to honor the vows of the covenant relationship, it grieves God. Marriage and family represents the total structure of your relationship with God; when you cannot, or do not honor the sanctity of holy matrimony; you grieve God. Favor comes upon those who are:

- Watching—looking for good things to happen
- Waiting for good things to happen
- Praying for good things to happen
- Keeping His Commands to ensure good things happen
- Walking in kindness and truth so as to not block good things from happening

All of these things produce favor!

The reason that many of us are missing blessings, our prayers are not answered, and we are not living in victory, is because we are not obedient to what the Word has to say. The source of our troubles is in our misunderstanding of what God expects of us, our reinterpretation of truth, or our blatant failure to do what is required.

We have made the distinction between grace and favor. Before we close, we need to understand the distinction between favor and faith. The word tells us that in faith we need to ask and believe to receive. However, we need to recognize that God can favor us apart from our faith. Sometimes favor works when faith will not or does not. Often we do not even know it, or even recognize it. Favor at times functions in the background of our faith, totally apart from our faith, setting us up for an unexpected outcome.

There have been times when you were in danger and do not know you were in danger. Let me illustrate.

- You were at the nightclub and someone starting shooting just after you left and an innocent by-stander was killed. You found favor that night. You might not have been looking for it, but that night at the club, you found favor. There was no faith involved because you never knew of the danger.
- You fell asleep at the wheel driving down the highway and you awakened just in time to avoid an accident. There was no faith involved because you didn't know you would go to sleep. You found favor.
- A storm hit and messed up every one else's car or house, but yours came out OK. There was no faith involved because you slept through the storm and heard on the news the next morning that a slight tornado had hit last night! You found favor.
- What about when your employer merged with another employer and you heard some folks would be laid off; you were found in God's favor, favor said "not you."
- What about those times when some young people went on a shooting rampage through the school; you were found in God's favor, favor said "not your child's school."

- What about when the doctor said you wouldn't make it through your sickness; he said surgery was a risk and you might not make it off the operating table; you were found in God's favor. Favor said, "Not time yet."
- What about the time the light bill was due and you received a shutoff notice. You were found in God's favor. Favor said, "We will leave the lights on for you."
- What about those times you were "sleeping around" during your player days. There were diseases to be caught but you missed them. You missed the STD and HIV (and you know you were some kind of awful in our heyday—let's be real). You were found in God's favor! I may be wrong, but I really do not think you had faith while you were out there sleeping around!

But what about faith?

- You have faith, but your money is still tight
- You have faith, but you are still sick
- You have faith; but granny is still in the hospital
- You have faith, but your marriage is still in trouble
- You have faith, but you still have to go to court
- You have faith, but the job still laid you off

Sometimes when it appears that you have had a faith failure, you just need to hang on. Sometimes what you ask for in faith; God will finish with favor! God still had to give favor in order for the transaction to be complete. Catch this:

- After your layoff, another job door opened
- In court the judge dismissed the charges
- Your husband or wife came home from church and God had spoken a life changing word in their spirit for your broken marriage
- You found out that new prescription was nursing granny back to good health
- You found out that favor had a high priority healing in your body
- You found out the favor had sent you an unexpected check in the mail

Even when we do not have the faith, God has the favor. Sometimes favor operates in the background of our wavering faith and favor sets us up for an unexpected outcome.

REFLECTIONS AND MEDITATIONS

1. Have you moved beyond the matter of salvation to seek God's favor?
2. As you reflect on the circumstances of your life, can you see the hand of God watching over you, protecting you, opening doors of opportunity for you?
3. Can you recognize the providence of God, His divine favor, in your relationship? In your daily affairs?

4. Are you living in such a manner that you can expect an outpouring of God's favor in your relationships?

PRAYER

Thank the Lord for His favor that is exercised on your behalf even when you don't realize that it is being done. Pray that as you walk in obedience you may grow in favor and faith.

Chapter 5

ALL ADVICE IS NOT GOOD ADVICE

We must weigh whatever advice we receive in terms of our own situation and in the light of God's Word.

"The plans of the righteous are just, but the advice of the wicked is deceitful." (Proverbs 12:5, NIV)

An old fable passed down for generations tells about an elderly man who was traveling with a boy and a donkey. As they walked through a village, the man was leading the donkey and the boy was walking behind. The townspeople said the old man was a fool for not riding, so to please them he climbed up on the animal's back. When they came to the next village, the people said the old man was cruel to let the child walk while he enjoyed the ride. So, to please them, he got off, set the boy on the animal's back, and continued on his way. In the third village, people accused the child of being lazy for making the old man walk, and the suggestion was made that they both ride. So the man climbed on and they set off again. In the fourth village, the townspeople were indignant at the cruelty to the donkey because he was made to carry two people. The frustrated man was last seen carrying the donkey down the road.

The world is full of those who would offer us advice. Everyone seems to have his or her opinion as to what is right or wrong, good or bad, relevant or irrelevant. An Old Danish proverb declares; He who builds according to every man's advice will have a crooked house. So, how do we discern what is best for us? When we ask for advice what is our motive? What is our goal? Some ask for advice but are not asking for an impartial opinion. They are actually looking for an accomplice, someone to agree with them and certify their decisions and behaviors.

Well-meaning Christians may offer us advice, and much of it is valuable. However, when we try to do everything other believers want us to do; we can easily become frustrated and confused.

When it comes to the matter of taking advice all advice is not good advice.

SOME DECISIONS ARE PERMANENT

In life, we need to be careful about the decisions we make because often it is hard, if not impossible, to go back, and undo some things. There are some things, which we have said and if we could, we would go back and unsay. Some things we have done and if we could, we would go back and undo. The reality is that some things said tend to burn permanent memories on the pallets of our minds and the minds of others. Some things done can cause permanent physical or emotional injury to others and us. Try as we may, some things that happen to us are hard, if not impossible to forget or forgive. Therefore, we must be very careful and not make rash decisions or statements. We must be careful not to operate our lives out of anger. When we are angry, that is not the time to make decisions about the rest of our lives, our mate, our job, or other significant issues. The bible says of anger:

> *"A hot-tempered man stirs up dissension, but a patient man calms a quarrel." (Proverbs 15:18, NIV)*

> *"Better a patient man than a warrior, a man who controls his temper than one who takes a city." (Proverbs 16:32, NIV)*

> *"Refrain from anger and turn from wrath; do not fret—it leads only to evil. For evil men will be cut off, but those who hope in the LORD will inherit the land." (Psalm 37:8-9, NIV)*

I wonder how many of our decisions are born of anger. Bad, stubborn, and proud decisions made as a result of anger rob us of a wonderful marriage or a relationship. How many of our harsh, foolish words have hardened into unbreakable laws, where we find ourselves helpless to change them, even though we know they're destroying our relationship?

SOME DECISIONS ARE MADE BY CIRCUMSTANCE

Many women and men go through life always looking for someone better: better physical features, better education, better financial position, better spiritual relationship, better, better, better. At some point, the quest for someone else that is better has to end. At some point, you have to resolve and come to grips with the reality of what attributes you possess. Sometimes the person God has blessed you with is possibly better than you deserve (smile), possibly better than you could ever find second time around.

At some point, we all have to make some decisions. Relationships are in many ways like going shopping. What I am about to say, please take it with sense of humor, and not too seriously:

- Some people like to window shop by going to the mall, just to be doing something. They never buy much, they just like to be in the atmosphere of the stores, and out with friends. If you are a shopper, if you never have any intention to marry, acknowledge it. Tell your friends and family that you will always be looking and never plan to enter into a permanent relationship so stop bugging you, and be OK with that.
- For some when to stop shopping may be a matter of your biological clock ticking, or getting up in age. You may have to weigh your choices and pick the best "baby daddy or baby momma" you can find or resolve that children are just not in God's plan for you.

- For others it may be all the models are appearing to look the same, a few features are better or worse, none of them fits the bill completely, and every year choices are fewer. You are getting tired of looking, your feet are beginning to hurt, the parties and clubs are getting old, and the dating game is no longer fun. You may just have to pray, pick the best one, and trust God that it will all work out in the end. Yes, at some point we all stop shopping.

The quest for stardom, the quest to be and have the best, be it in our employment, acquisition of things and stuff, spiritual growth, marital relations can become unrealistic unless we have a real sense of who we are. Some people spend an entire lifetime discontent with where they are, always looking for a star to grasp onto, always looking for a better job, a better mate, a better this, a better that, and never learn to appreciate where and with whom God has placed them. Sometimes it is only in illness that some come to appreciate their spouse and their situation.

We often presume that there is someone better out there and that presumption often leads to dissatisfaction in our relationships.

SOME DECISIONS PUT US IN DANGER

In the relationship the characters of Mista and Celie had in the *Color Purple*, he said and she did. Whatever he said went. She couldn't even go and fetch the mail.

Celie gave Harpo, her son, some bad advice when he was having trouble being respected by his wife Sophia. She told him to beat her. Harpo tried that with Sophia and found himself with a black eye (Sophia said, "I loves Harpo; God knows I do, but I kill him dead before I let him beat me.") Other men have taken the advice of others and tried to legislate respect in their homes. Remember the singer Al Green. Maybe Al Green tried that, or something similar, and that's why he found himself covered with hot grits. Those of us who are 21st century men, Christian men, know that trying to legislate respect, or in a spiritual sense, trying to legislate holiness in our homes, does not work. Marriage is a partnership. It runs best when there is mutual respect and cooperation.

Respect is not something that can be legislated; it is something that must be earned. Holiness is not something that can be legislated; it is something that must be lived out. You cannot legislate that you are the head of your household, because unless your wife agrees and allows you to adopt your biblical role, you will always have a house in conflict. You will be at odds like Harpo and Sophia, always in some state of turmoil, either physical or emotional. You can only be as much head of your household as your wife allows you to be. We need to keep our ego in check!

SOME ADVISORS ARE WORSE OFF THAN THOSE THEY ADVISE

You have to be careful about taking advice from people whose lives don't line up with their testimony, who lives are more messed up than your own. If you are trying to find healing for your relationship, you need to be careful who you are talking to, and from whom you are getting advice. Some people are in emotionally bad places where they have been hurt and have not climbed out of the hole of depression, anger, remorse, or abuse. Any advice from them will be colored by the setting and atmosphere of their relationship, their own present and past hurts, and drama. Yes, oftentimes when you go to someone for advice, or even share in casual conversation, you will find they have more issues than you do, and you end up counseling him or her. Pick those to whom you go for advice carefully. Some advice ought to carry the warning: "DO NOT TRY THIS AT HOME!" We must weigh whatever advice we receive in terms of our own situation and in the light of God's Word.

GOOD ADVICE IS SPIRITUAL ADVICE

If you want to have a healthy earthly relationship, you need to have a healthy heavenly relationship. Unless you are caught-up in a love triangle with the Father and the Son, you are caught-up in the wrong love triangle. A love triangle with the Father and the Son, held together by the spiritual glue of the Holy Spirit will keep you from compromising your integrity, from thoughts of someone else's wife, from investing in dead-end and dead-beat relationships, and from hanging onto senseless hopes and dreams of living happily ever after.

Unless you are grounded in truth and obedience to God's Word, whatever the status of your earthly relationship, you are caught-up in a sinful and destructive triangle that will lead you down a road to pain, the kind of pain that eventually reaps the harvest of sin from seeds that have been sown. Unless Jesus is the third member of your relationship, your love, life, and sexuality, you are fooling yourself with thoughts of living happily ever after.

Those in favor of common law marriages will say of legal marriage that it is "just a piece of paper," and for some it probably is. If however that is true, if it is "just a piece of paper," why not get married? The fact is that they recognize it is more than just a piece of paper. That piece of paper commits two people to a deep relationship legally, spiritually, financially, and morally. Those who say it is just a piece of paper sincerely recognize that once they sign on that line it becomes much more than just a piece of paper. It legally and morally binds them to a relationship with a person from whom they cannot just walk away without consequences. That's why they want to pass it off as just a piece of paper. It is more than just a piece of paper; it is a legal and binding contract. If someone claims to truly love you, and he or she is not willing to be legally bound to you that is not the kind of

- Love that you want
- Person you want for your "baby daddy" or "baby momma."
- Person you want to become legally entangled with in buying houses and cars
- Person with whom you want to invest the best part of your life

That kind of a love is a fearful love, a timid love, a tentative love, a creating a back door to get out of it love.

If you are living with someone else's wife, or someone else's husband, living with someone else's significant other, or in a sexual relationship outside of marriage, recognize that God is left out. Again, if God is left out, you will eventually reap the harvest of sin from seeds that has been sown, and be assured that you will not live happily ever after.

The story is told of a child who stood gazing at a freshly opened box of chocolates. With her lower lip bitten by her upper teeth, a frown of concentration wrinkled the space between her dark eyebrows; she held her breath in fear of making an unchangeable mistake. She had been told, "only one Jessica, no more than one—anyone you want, but you may have only one. Choose." Should it be the biggest one, or might that small round one be the favorite peppermint cream? Then again, the long one could be nougat and that would last longer. It was an agonizing choice to be made in the next few minutes of time.

We all have to make choices in this world, choices that determine our future and which often cannot be changed. We must be careful in seeking counsel that we seek those who can help us to make decisions that are beneficial for us in the areas of our spiritual life as well as our physical life.

The challenge before us today as Christians is to align the moral tone and spiritual goals of our lives with God. Unbelievers may advise us that it is not fashionable. Some friends may advise us that to put our faith in God is not a good investment.

One thing we know for sure, there is no danger in choosing God. There is never a wrong choice in choosing to serve God.

REFLECTIONS AND MEDITATIONS

1. How do you determine the creditability of those who offer you advice?
2. How do your emotions figure in the decisions that you make? Are you able to separate the emotion of the situation from the decision that needs to be made?
3. Do you allow you circumstances to determine your decision or are you able to look at the larger picture?
4. How does God figure into decisions made regarding your relationship? Is He the third member in the triangle of your relationship?

PRAYER

Ask the Lord to help you discern between truth and error, to be led of His Spirit and not of your flesh, and that He may be the third person who speaks into every relationship of your life.

Chapter 6

THE BIBLE IS OUR BEST SOURCE OF ADVICE

In Deuteronomy 17:14-20, Moses gives advice to the Children of Israel regarding the choice of a king. In retrospect, we can see if Solomon had given heed to this admonition, he would not have fallen victim to the seductive influence of his wives, followed other gods, and abused his wealth.

14 *"When you come to the land which the Lord your God is giving you, and possess it and dwell in it, and say, `I will set a king over me like all the nations that are around me,'*

15 *"you shall surely set a king over you whom the Lord your God chooses; one from among your brethren you shall set as king over you; you may not set a foreigner over you, who is not your brother.*

16 "But he shall not multiply horses for himself, nor cause the people to return to Egypt to multiply horses, for the Lord has said to you, `You shall not return that way again.'

17 "Neither shall he multiply wives for himself, lest his heart turn away; nor shall he greatly multiply silver and gold for himself.

Although God blessed Solomon with great and extravagant wealth, it appears that it may have become his downfall. If Solomon had given sincere attention to Moses advice and forewarning, he would have been kept from error. Clearly, the Word of God was intended to be the source of continuing wisdom for the people of God.

18 "Also it shall be, when he sits on the throne of his kingdom, that he shall write for himself a copy of this law in a book, from the one before the priests, the Levites.

19 "And it shall be with him, and he shall read it all the days of his life, that he may learn to fear the Lord his God and be careful to observe all the words of this law and these statutes,

20 "that his heart may not be lifted above his brethren, that he may not turn aside from the commandment to the right hand or to the left, and that he may prolong his days in his kingdom, he and his children in the midst of Israel.

Whether or not he generated a copy of the law, we are not certain. What we do know is that he failed to apply it in the area of his marital relationships and his wealth.

The Bible is what many have called the "owners manual" for those of us who are Christians. It covers the operation of our lives from birth to death, tells us what to do when we have erratic situations, gives us troubleshooting tips for problems, answers FAQ's (frequently asked questions), and generally informs us as to how to make the most productive use of this body.

However, we live in an age where many of our daily life operations are intuitive, meaning that we make it up, figure it out, or formulate solutions to situations as we go through life. Just as with computer software, cell phones, and video games, we know that if played with long enough we can get the hang of it. A quicker way is to ask someone who has the same program, phone, or game specific questions as to its operation. Rather than reading the instructions, many of us go through life intuitively. We rarely take the time to read the instructions for ourselves.

Yes, many of us are passing through this life anticipating, responding, and living our lives on an intuitive basis. Responding to life situations the way we think they ought to be, justifying what is done along life's pathway, or obtaining input from other people. The reality is that the Bible is meant for each of us to read personally. It is self-described as a living Word. Hebrews 4:12 declares,

> *"For the word of God is living and powerful, and sharper than any two-edged sword, piercing even*

> *to the division of soul and spirit, and of joints and marrow, and is a discerner of the thoughts and intents of the heart."*

When it comes to the Bible, we do not take the time to read the manual that tells us of the proper manner to live. The Bible would speak to our intuitive mentality this way, Proverbs 14:12 declares, *"There is a way that seems right to a man, but its end is the way of death."* Additionally, Proverbs 21:2 declares, *"Every way of a man is right in his own eyes, but the Lord weighs the hearts."* We cannot trust ourselves, or be led by our own instincts. They will always betray us. They will lead us astray. Isaiah 53:6 informs us that *"All we like sheep have gone astray; we have turned, every one, to his own way. . ."*

The problem with trying to figure life out on our own is that valuable information can remain hidden from us, which can help us to operate more efficiently, experience less frustration in life, and show us exactly what life is all about. 2 Timothy 3:16-17 declares,

> *"All Scripture is given by inspiration of God, and is profitable for doctrine, for reproof, for correction, for instruction in righteousness, that the man of God may be complete, thoroughly equipped for every good work."*

Someone has said, "A Bible that's falling apart probably belongs to someone who isn't."

If the Bible could speak and apply for a job as the advisor of your life, it might say the following:

> "I would like a job as tutor, teacher, and advisor to your family. I will never take a vacation. I will never be out of humor. I don't drink or smoke. I won't borrow your clothes or raid your refrigerator. I will be up in the morning as early as anyone in the household and will stay up as late as anyone wishes. I will help solve any problems your children might have. I will give you the satisfaction of knowing that no question your children ask will go unanswered. For that matter, I will answer any of your own questions on subjects that range from 'How we got here?' to 'Where are we headed?' I will help settle bets and differences of opinion. I will give you information that will help you with your job, your family, and all of your other interests. In short, I will give you the knowledge that will insure the continued success of your family. I am your Bible. Do I get the job?"

One day, a teacher was teaching her young class the story of Jesus visiting Mary and Martha. She carefully explained how Mary and Martha had hurried to clean the house and cook a special meal. Then she paused and asked, "What would you do if Jesus was going to visit your house today?" One little girl quickly responded, "I'd put the Bible on the table!"

In times like these, we are called to consider, has the Bible, the book of law, fallen into disuse? We all have at least one bible in our homes. Some of us have multiple bibles, versions, leather-bound, paperback, big print, study, and other distinctions. However, they are a part of the spiritual décor of our homes, but not the spiritual foundation of our lives.

If we are going to find good advice it is not going to be because we stumble upon it somewhere, but because we are busy, doing what we know is right, because we are honoring God with our lives, we have an appreciation for His Word, and foster a desire to read it.

We need to rediscover its claims, its promises, and its procedures for leading a productive life. We need to be convicted of the need to clean some stuff out of our lives if we are going to walk in obedience to God's Word. We can only do better when we know better. Knowing better requires that we know the truth, the Word of God for ourselves.

1 Corinthians 2:14-16 tells us that understanding can only come out of a relationship with Jesus Christ.

> *"But the natural man does not receive the things of the Spirit of God, for they are foolishness to him; nor can he know them, because they are spiritually discerned. But he who is spiritual judges all things, yet he himself is rightly judged by no one. For "who has known the mind of the Lord that he may instruct Him?" But we have the mind of Christ."*

The first priority is to know Christ, because we can only begin to understand the Bible if we are in relationship with him.

Let us not live this life intuitively, that is operating according to what we think, responding to the cues that life gives us, or following the direction of those who are supposedly in-the-know. Let us read the directions for ourselves! Only then will we be able to know and follow the best advice.

REFLECTIONS AND MEDITATIONS

1. What part does the Bible play in the daily routine of your life? Have you established a daily regime of reading the Word of God?
2. In reflection, what bad decisions have you made, or what circumstances have subtly crept into your life that the Bible clearly warns against?

PRAYER

Pray that the Word of God may be your first source of wisdom and advice, and that you may weigh all other human opinions against His truth.

Chapter 7

A CLOSING WORD OF ADVICE

Everybody ends up somewhere in life. A few people end up somewhere on purpose. It takes vision to end up somewhere on purpose. God has placed you somewhere on purpose. What you are doing, where you are located, at this point in your life, is no accident. You may not know what God is up to behind the scenes of your life, but you are positioned for purpose. It may be difficult to see the connection now. However, in time, it will come together.

God is using your present circumstances to prepare you to accomplish His vision for your life. Your present circumstances are part of the vision. You are not wasting your time in serving God. You are not spinning your wheels in exercising the daily spiritual disciplines of life. You are not wandering in the wilderness. If you are *"seeking first" his kingdom"* (Matthew 6:33) where you are, then where you are is where he has positioned you. And he has positioned you there with a purpose in mind. It may be difficult for you to make the connection at this point. However, if you are patient, in time, God will reveal His will for your life.

Seek good advice, but remember that God is the one is the source of all good advice and ultimately decides the course for your life. We have the assurance that God intends and desires good for us.

> *"For I know the thoughts that I think toward you, says the Lord, thoughts of peace and not of evil, to give you a future and a hope." (Jeremiah 29:11)*

> *"I have come that they may have life, and that they may have it more abundantly. (John 10:10)*

FOR SINGLES

Some would naively say, it is a woman's business to get married as soon as possible and a man's to keep unmarried as long as he can.

If you are single, the unbelieving world and even those within the community of believers, often try to impose upon you that you are somehow inadequate, that you not being married somehow makes you less than complete. That unless you get married true happiness will never be yours.

The reality is there are those who in all honesty would tell you "I never knew what real happiness was until I got married." It was not that they found it in marriage, but realized how blessed they were in being single. Some have come to be married only to find it a living hell. Some regard marriage as a goal to be reached at all expense. Many who fall into love seem to fall out of their senses at the same time. They display infinitely more anxiety to get married than they do to get to heaven. Evidently, they regard it as a most precious paradise, but when they reach it by the road of folly and sexual compromise; they generally find that it is bittersweet. When not founded on the right foundation, contrary to Solomon's declaration of it being a good thing, it can be filled with nothing but turmoil.

Many singles are missing a blessing because they are more interested in the outside wrapper than in the contents of the package, more interested in what kinds of clothes he or she wears, or what kind of car he or she drives, or where he or she works than in what kind of person he or she is. You cannot build a relationship on those things, you need to not only look at the container but also look at the contents. For no matter how pretty or handsome the container may be, the contents may be something you do not want. When you go grocery shopping your concern is not how pretty the containers will look on your shelf but what is within them. If you do not have good contents no matter how good the container looks you will still go hungry. Many now are in bad marriages because they married containers and not contents. You can work with good contents, you can shape and mold it and make it, not matter what the container looks like. Singles I'm not saying as it was sung in the 60's, "If your want to be happy for the rest of your life, make an ugly woman (man) your wife (your husband)." But what I am saying is to have an eye which can discern the potential of person.

Some of the most frustrated Christians in God's family are those who are single in desperate search of a mate. They come in both sexes, all sizes, any age, different circumstances, and they often live on the anxious edge of panic and fear. As a result, their lives are counting little for eternity, and their eyes are frequently upon themselves. Many singles are emotional basket cases because they cannot find anybody. This anxiety accounts for the growing population of single's bars and (dare we admit it) single adult fellowship groups within our churches.

The Bible's advice to those who are desperately hunting for a mate is simply, "stop." Instead, invest that same energy in growing close to the Lord. He knows far better where your husband or wife is than you do.

If God intends for you to marry, you will meet your future mate only when the Lord's appointed time arrives. Nothing you can do will make that day arrive any sooner. So why waste precious time in a futile and demeaning search that leaves you feeling unloved, unwanted, and unsuccessful? Why not use those days, months, or years to deepen your walk with God and grow more mature as an individual. Both of these endeavors will make you more attractive to that future spouse when you eventually meet. And the time in between will be productive and satisfying. Instead of trying to find a mate, seek the Lord!

1. Transfer your energy into other endeavors (physical, mental, etc.)
2. Seek to love and be loved and put marriage secondary
3. Let go of the sensual temptations of the world
4. Reprogram your mind with divine truth

5. Receive that God has chosen you to live without sex for the moment
6. Avoid dangerous situations
7. Thank and praise God for the situation you are in

Whatever the circumstances and no matter how strong the bond of love; whenever two sinners start living under the same roof; there is going to be trouble. (Can't you just hear the chorus of married people saying, "Amen!") The same man who held the door for his adoring sweetheart will someday slam the door as he leaves for work in huff. The same blushing bride who cries for joy when her man brings her flowers will so day sob in self-pity when forgets her birthday again. Even good marriages (as rare as they are) take their toll on your patience.

Without trying to give a distorted view of marriage, there is something far worse than living alone. It is being bound to someone who adds to your problems instead of relieving them. It is to the troubles of adjustment, disagreements, responsibilities, and demand of marriage.

FOR THOSE MARRIED

The story is told of a woman who wasn't happy in her marriage. So she went to see her psychologist, Dr. George Crane. And she said, "Dr Crane, I hate my husband. I don't appreciate the way he treats me. I want a divorce! And I want to hurt him as much as I can."

Dr Crane said, "Well, if you really want to hurt him, this is what you should do. Start showering him with compliments. Tell him you love him. What a good husband he is. And how after all these years, you're glad you married him. Write him little notes of appreciation. And after a few months, when he thinks everything is going great, start the divorce action."

So she did everything he suggested. A few months later, she went back to Dr. Crane. And he said, "Well, are you ready to file for divorce?" She said, "Divorce? Why would I want to do that? I love my husband!" You see, once she performed the actions of love. The feelings of love all came back. If you have lost your love for your good thing, devote yourself to giving your spouse creative, loving attention, you would be surprised at how fast the feelings could come back. Obviously, that was good advice!

Some of you may feel as if your marriage has depreciated to where it is worth little or nothing, and maybe it has. That in some ways may be good. If your marriage has bottomed out then anything you put into it can only make it better. The passion can be reclaimed. Nothing is impossible with God and with God involved in your relationship, nothing is impossible in a marriage. If God could raise Jesus Christ from the dead, he can certainly raise your marriage from the dead. But you have to give it a chance, stick it out, and make some efforts. The choice is yours.

A marital relationship involves intimacy. Intimacy means connection from the innermost areas. In its simplest form, we might say that it means "into-me-see." Biblical intimacy involves the whole person. Biblical intimacy is one of transparency with God and with our spouse. To be truly intimate with God we must open up our lives before God, sharing all our sin, faults, thoughts, ugliness, etc. We are as intimate with God as we choose to be.

We are as intimate with our spouse as we choose to be. To be intimate with our spouse we must be willing to risk giving ourselves totally, loving in spite of, and prayerfully seeking God's intervention in areas of difficulty.

God's unconditional love is proven by the sacrifice of His Son on our behalf. He loves us completely. If you want to rekindle your relationship, the first and best thing you can do for your marriage is to make Jesus Christ Lord of your life. Philippians 2:2 says, *"Fulfill my joy by being like-minded, having the same love, being of one accord, of one mind."*

Cassette tapes and Compact Discs of these messages are available.

William is available for preaching, workshops, conferences, and other ministry events.

You may learn more about William Golson by visiting: www.truelightonline.org

William may be personally contacted by e-mail:

revgolson@aol.com

Or:

William T. Golson, Jr.
P.O. Box 39003
Denver, CO 80239-0003

Other Publications by the Author:

"On the Matter of Relationships" (Xulon Press 2007)

"Adjusting Your Copy Quality: Becoming Who the Word Says You Are" (Xulon Press 2007